Desert Rose

Book One of the Broken Flowers

Series

By

Scarlett J Rose

ISBN: 978-0-6480098-2-5

Follow Scarlett J Rose on

Facebook:

https://www.facebook.com/scarlettjrose/

Thank-you:

To My Editor, Susan Horsnell, for taking the time to go through and do the awesome job you do.

To my Beta Readers, Kate McDonough, Cassandra Exley, Treena Ross, Kim Hankerson, Jess Barncastle, Darlene Tallman, Erika Escariz, Denise Baumann, Lyssa Reyome, Christine Raine Jalili, Chelle Johnette Keeton, Cindy Chessler and Hayfaah Sumtally. Thank you all for your time and input!

-Scarlett J Rose January 2017

Desert Rose.

Scarlett J Rose.

I was seventeen when my father gave my hand to the Devil...

I'd felt his eyes watching me throughout the night as I danced with my friends. My long skirt swirled around my legs, I felt vibrant and bright with merriment. I was unaware of the hunger my body had brought forth from the monster across the village square as the party for my father's birthday continued into the night.

I stopped dancing to check on my mother and see if she needed anything. Her body had become so frail since cancer had set in. I lived in hope she could fight the deadly tumour in her stomach, we were barely able to afford the treatments she so desperately needed. I had taken work at the nearby school, helping the young, handsome teacher with the little ones. My dream was to be a teacher one day. I'm smart enough to go to college and finished my schooling early. But for money and my mother's illness, I would have been studying to achieve my dream. Perhaps when she was well again, I could study.

My dream was shattered when my father joined me by my mother's side.

"Rosa." I gazed up at my beloved Papi.

He spared Mamá a loving glance. His eyes glistened with sadness and fear for his wife of so many years.

"Yes, Papi?" His weathered face reflected a somber hope that I didn't recognize, but took for concern over Mamá's condition.

"A very important guest wishes to meet you, my little one." He smiled, reaching up to tuck an errant strand of hair behind my ear.

I nodded my agreement, and being a good, dutiful daughter, I allowed him to take my hand and followed him meekly. Eduardo, the teacher I was working for, and who had captured my heart, watched me from a table nearby. I turned and gave him, what I hoped was a cheeky wink. After the party; I had promised him we would have some time together. It was time which my young heart beat furiously for, and I felt my cheeks heat in anticipation.

Papi stopped in front of an impressive man. He was at least ten years my senior and I knew he was of the local Cartel. The gold-plated pistols snuggled in their holsters at his hips were telling. Not to mention the four oversized men who stood casually, but alert nearby.

"Rosa, this is Señor Rivas, he has requested to meet you." Papi led me to a seat by the man's side. I let my eyes drift over him. He was handsome, rugged, muscled and exuded danger and excitement. I had noticed many of my older friends casting their pretty eyes his way. I could not understand why he would wish to spend a moment of his valuable time with me when there were much prettier girls at Papi's party.

"Rosa." He spoke my name and a wave of darkness and foreboding washed over me. "Such a beautiful name for a delicate flower." He leaned forward, placing the glass clutched in his hand on a table next to him. His hand took possession of mine, fingers and palm cold and damp from condensation on the glass. He lifted his hand, taking my knuckles to his perfect lips for a featherlight kiss. His dark eyes locked with mine. Inwardly I cringed, but outwardly I smiled and lowered my eyes. A show of shyness, my defense against this man.

His dark, deep voice asked questions of my youth, my life and my family. I answered him honestly, except when he asked me if I had a boyfriend. It was my first mistake, my first lie. Though even now, I don't think it would have made much of a difference in the way he pursued me for himself.

The band started to play the tune for *Happy Birthday* as my aunts brought out my father's birthday cake. Friends and family gathered around the long table in the center of our little village's square, crowding around the beautiful cake. We are not a rich family, but we are well-respected.

I was beckoned to my father's side and gracefully left Señor Rivas' company to return to the perceived safety of my family. Mamá, Papi, my elder brother, Ricardo, and Juan, my younger brother. We stood beside my parents and smiled lovingly at the devoted couple. I had always wanted to find a love such as theirs. My eyes flicked to Eduardo, and I couldn't help but smile at him.

"My friends, I am not a wealthy man…" My father began his speech. "But, I have been given the riches of love, family, friends and good health. I am blessed to have three wonderful and intelligent children and a woman who has made my life complete. If I were to die this night, I would go before God and thank him for everything I have been gifted in this life. I would go to my rest a content and happy man." He raised his glass of tequila, the flickering lights of the colorful lanterns refracting in the liquid. "For my friends, I wish you the very same, love, family, friends and good health. Thank you all for celebrating on this happy occasion." I watched as everyone downed their tequila in the toast with my father.

I drank watered down liquor; it was all I was allowed at this night. My eyes met those of Eduardo. He winked, knowing our time was coming close. The party would soon grow in its festivities. Alcohol would flow and revellers would become drunker. We would then slip away.

I returned to dance with my friends. My father sat with Señor Rivas and they spoke quietly. Señor Rivas' eyes darted to watch me every so often. Once, my eyes met his as I spun in dance, his fathomless gaze catching me as I swayed to the beautiful music. I did not know then, but I had

unintentionally enraptured him, and it would
change my life.

The Devil wanted me for his bride

Chapter Two

A week after my father's party, they came for me....

Mamá was seated in her chair in the kitchen, sobbing when I came home from work. My hair was wrapped up in a linen scarf. The hem of my dress dirty from the dusty road I walked to and from school. My face still heated from the stolen moments with Eduardo in the school's small supplies room.

His lips had captured my nipple as I exposed my breasts to him at his begging. His fingers slid between the lips of my pussy and teased me until I panted and begged for him to take me. I had turned eighteen the previous day and was now considered a woman. I hadn't wanted to wait for marriage like a good girl, I wanted the man I loved to claim me. The slight pain I felt at the intrusion of his manhood was nothing compared to the bliss he had brought to me while the school children were out at play.

His hand clamped over my mouth to muffle my moans. I cried out my final rapture as his seed entered me. We cleaned each other up, my mouth tasting the combined mixture of our love and the taint of my virginal blood as I cleaned him. Eduardo had taken the clean handkerchief he had on him at all times and cleaned between my legs, showing me the smear of blood, which remained.

I watched as he slipped the handkerchief in his pocket, thanking me for the gift of my virginity. It was then he sank to bended knee and proposed. He had no ring yet, but he had his heart and love eternal to offer me. My heart soared, tears of joy flowed down my cheeks. Though Eduardo was four years older than I, I loved

him with all my heart and knew we would
be happy together.

Ricardo sat with Mamá and smiled
sadly at me. "Go wash up, Rosa. Papi wishes
to speak with you. Wear your prettiest
dress." Mamá gazed up at me with tear-
filled eyes.

"What's happened, Mamá? Is
everything all right?" I knelt before her. I
feared she had bad news to give me.

She shook her head and dabbed at
her eyes. "Something wonderful has
happened, my little one. Now hurry, Papi is
waiting."

I kissed her tear-stained cheek,
tasting the salt of her tears on my lips, not
realizing I would become familiar with the
acidic taste of my own very soon.

I hurried to the backyard and washed my face at the old hand pump my father kept working. Plumbing in our village is rare and reserved for those who can afford it. Keeping Mamá's medical bills paid, and food on our table, was more important than a luxury such as indoor plumbing.

Even in this modern era of airplanes, computers and satellites, we still had an outhouse and carried in water for our baths from the old pump. I scrubbed my face, using the linen scarf which bound my hair to pat the droplets of water from my skin. I ran a hand through my hair, tousling the long, dark tresses as my mind pondered every possibility which would require attending my father in my prettiest dress.

I hurried to the small room that was mine alone. I changed into my red polka-dot dress, by far the prettiest one Mamá had made for me. Designer clothes were an indulgence for most in the village, and the women were capable seamstresses. Bolts of fabric were bought in the larger towns and brought back to the village to be sewn into wearable clothes. Yes, we are rustic in our ways, but we find it more satisfying than wasting vast amounts on frivolous clothes which were likely to wear out within a week.

I ran my grandmother's silver brush through my hair, a gift from her on her deathbed. It was the only thing I had to remember her by. She died a poor widow, reliant on my mother's care. She took her last breaths in the room I now call my own. The brush had been used by my grandmother to untangle my hair before I left for school every morning. One day I came home to find her lying as if asleep on the bed, her body was cold, and I couldn't awaken her. It was my first experience with death. It would not be my last, but by far the most peaceful.

I froze with the brush in mid-air when a thought hit me. Eduardo must have asked my father for my hand in marriage before he proposed. I couldn't help the grin which parted my lips. I hurriedly searched the small chest at the end of my bed and dabbed on the perfume Ricardo had given me for my sixteenth birthday. I applied a small amount of makeup to my face, being careful not to look like a cheap hooker in the process. I slipped my feet into black ballet flats and checked myself in the cracked mirror on the wall.

A young woman was reflected. A face flushed with life and excitement for the future peered back. I blew a kiss to myself and left my small room. I headed to the living room, bypassing the kitchen where Ricardo and Mamá were sitting, drinking coffee. I stopped at the closed door of the living room, knocked softly and smiled.

The stranger who opened the door had a presence which made me want to take a step back. I had seen him before at my father's birthday party. He was one of Señor Rivas' bodyguards.

I glanced around him into the room. Sitting on Mamá's sofa, sipping coffee in her best porcelain cup, was Señor Rivas. A proud, and possessive, smile plastered his face as the door opened and I was allowed into the living room.

Papi stood and approached me, pride evident on his face. "Rosa." He opened his arms and gathered me in a loving, fatherly embrace. Rivas stood as well, nodding amicably to me, I smiled nervously and returned his greeting. Papi invited me to sit on the sofa, I did so reluctantly. Rivas waited until I was seated and, to my horror, sat beside me. His eyes devoured me possessively.

"Rosa, Señor Rivas has come here today, to ask me for your hand in marriage. It is a proposal I have accepted."

Papi's words shattered my perfect world, my plans for a happily ever after. The fairy-tale dream I had nursed since I was fifteen of becoming a teacher, and now Eduardo's wife changed instantly into a heart-shattering nightmare.

"But… Papi…" My throat choked up, the tightness ensuring no other words were able to find their way into the air.

Papi lifted his hand to hush me, a smile on his face. "My beautiful daughter, Mr. Rivas has offered to pay for your mother's treatments in the best hospital in the city. His only request is the hand of my loving daughter."

Papi smiled at Señor Rivas as the man placed his hand over my trembling fingers. He lifted my hand to his lips. My mouth wide, agape in shock.

"Rosa, your father has accepted my proposal, we will be married tomorrow." His hands gripped my own. "I will give you everything you ever dreamed of, you will have beautiful clothes, good food, and your mother will be healthy, happy, especially when we give her beautiful grandchildren." His smile was pure evil. I lowered my head as I felt my eyes sting with tears for everything I had lost.

"You will be happy." Rivas placed his fingers under my chin and raised my face to meet his. He leaned forward and pressed his lips against mine. There was a dark passion behind the kiss. His tongue slid out and caressed my lips. He tasted of mint.

It was a taste of fate. Of broken promises, and shattered dreams.

The Devil lied……..

Chapter Three

I felt caught in a waking nightmare. Rivas, whose first name was Emmanuel, took me gently by the hand and guided me to the kitchen, where my Mamá kissed both my cheeks, giving me her blessing. I was numb to the very core of my being.

In the course of one afternoon, I had given the man I loved my virginity, and accepted his proposal, only to come home to find my father had accepted a proposal on my behalf from another man. One who was rich, immeasurably dangerous, and had ties to a deadly cartel. It wasn't until we were driving away from my home the reality of the situation hit me. I felt the first hot tear trickle down my cheek. Emmanuel's finger slid across my skin, capturing the errant tear, wiping it away.

"Do not fret, my pretty bride. All will be well. You will be happy with me as a husband." He relaxed back in his seat.

I leaned against the hot glass of the car's window, watching as the little village, my home, rushed past in a near blur. Eduardo was out the front of the small teacher's house at the school, sweeping the dirt from the porch. He glanced up and saw my face in the car's window. The broom fell from his hands. I placed my hand to the window, my eyes begging him for help, unable to call out for him to save me from my fate.

Beside me, Emmanuel leaned forward, following my line of sight as we drove past the school. He turned his head as we passed the school and my first lover. His dark eyes narrowed as Eduardo stepped onto the road to watch the car disappear.

Emmanuel sat back, casually reaching into his pocket to pull out a silver cigarette case. I detested smoking, even banishing Ricardo to the backyard with the broom when he tried to light up a cigarette in the house. I heard the ignition of the flint of a lighter and saw the golden flare of a flame as Emmanuel lit up the tobacco. His next words drove a shiver down my spine.

"So, who is the teacher to you? Or, more accurately, who *was* the teacher to you?" His voice was casual and calm, but the deadly threat could not be mistaken.

"A friend." My voice was barely above a whisper.

His hand slid into the tresses of my hair and gripped the strands close to my scalp. I squealed in pain as he pulled me back, hard against his body. "A friend, you say, Rosa, my love?" His voice was laced with anger next to my ear. I smelled the stench of cigarette smoke and saw it curling from his lips and nostrils. "More than a friend, I think." His hand shook me in warning. "For every lie that passes your lips, I will dedicate a bullet for his body."

"He is my boyfriend." I whispered.

"That's two bullets, my love."

"Two…?" I gasped, my eyes widened in horror.

"Yes, at your father's birthday party, you told me you did not have a boyfriend. That was the first lie. The second was you telling me he was just a friend." His tongue darted out and swiped at an errant tear, catching it, savoring it like a fine wine. He smiled, lips curling in victory. "Is there anything else you wish to tell me?"

I shook my head. I refused to place the man I loved, or my family in any further danger.

"Good. There are only three things I require of you as my wife; loyalty, obedience and honesty." He released my hair, but slid an arm around my waist, pulling me tight against his hard body. I lowered my head and allowed my tears of grief to fall freely. I felt empty, alone, and afraid of the monster who sat beside me. And, I had no doubt, the man was also dangerous, evil.

I wish my father had known the Devil had attended his party.

Chapter Four

I was deposited at a luxury hotel with two of Rivas' men watching over me while he conducted business in the city. I dared not ask him what his business was. I had watched as he checked the golden plated guns, ensuring their clips were filled with bullets. He removed two of the deadly leads and smiled darkly at me; he was reminding me of his promise. Every lie that passed my lips would grant another bullet to Eduardo's body.

He left me with the two guards for most of the night, returning in the early hours of the morning. A woman's cheap perfume wafted from him causing my nose to wrinkle in disgust and my eyes to water. I lay in the bed, listening to his movements in the bathroom as he readied for bed.

The sounds of running water in the basin, the shower, the sound of him urinating, and the subsequent flush of the toilet, and again the basin as he washed up afterward. The light switch clicked as he left the bathroom, the glow dying and leaving the room in darkness but for the small lamp in the sitting area where his goon lounged. Emmanuel dismissed the man, waiting until the suite's door closed before slipping into bed beside me.

His hands were rough, calloused as they slid over my almost naked body. I had climbed into bed wearing my bra and panties, though I had covered myself with one of the bathrobes supplied by the hotel. His hands were hot against my body, raising gooseflesh over my skin. I felt my hair being pulled aside as his lips descended onto the curve of my shoulder, moving up to my neck.

"Rosa, is there anything else I should know, anything you wish to tell me? Consider this your last chance." He unclasped my bra and stroked the skin at my back. I bit my lip, unable to speak for the fear thundering through my body. He pushed me onto my back and I trembled as he pulled down my panties and placed himself over me, his knees forcing my own apart.

We had not even said our wedding vows and he was mounting me like the whores he had visited. They had obviously not slaked his lust. I whimpered as he entered me, slowly, but steadily. His cock was thick, larger than Eduardo's and he took me roughly. The velvet soft skin of my pussy screamed in protest as he tore the delicate folds. I was dry, unaroused, not eager and unwilling. But, I had no choice. The lives of my beloved Eduardo, and perhaps even my family, hung by a thread that Emmanuel Rivas could sever at any moment.

"So tight," he grunted as he thrust inside me. "So sweet. Are you a virgin, my lovely?" I knew he wasn't expecting me to answer when he laughed knowingly. I turned my head to the side, ignoring the lips which descended to my neck, my jawline.

He slipped a hand beneath my cheek and turned my head to him insistantly. His lips traced mine with butterfly kisses which would have melted my heart had I loved him. Instead, they felt like slimy caterpillars crawling over my mouth. His tongue darted out, a vile slippery slug slithering its way between my lips as he thrust harder inside me. He grunted, panted and moaned as I lay beneath him. My soul soared to a place where I was happy; Eduardo was the groom whom I would meet in the morning in my white dress. The man who would take me to the sweet little house at the school where we would teach the village's children and raise our little ones in happiness and peace.

The searing heat of his semen and the weight of his sweaty, muscular body jerked me back to the reality of my life. I felt him pull himself free of my body, a sticky trail following his slowly sagging penis. His lips found mine, and I forced myself not to recoil as he tasted me. He climbed from the bed and padded to the bathroom to clean himself up. I rolled over, and my tears fell and soaked the pillow beneath my head.

I drifted off into a sleep filled with misery and woeful dreams of a life I could never have, Eduardo standing proudly beside me as we watched our children play.

I woke up alone, but for Riva's goon, sitting in the chair, watching me with a wry grin on his face. There were three bullets on

the table where last night, there had been
two.

The Devil had known I was not pure.

Chapter Five.

I stood looking at myself in the mirror. Beautiful white silk covered my tanned skin. My mother fussed around me with my aunts and adjusted the skirt or my bust in the figure-hugging dress.

The dress was *off the rack* of an expensive boutique in the city. Rivas had insisted on making the choice for me. A veil with white satin roses adorned my head and the world was shaded in white as the veil draped over my face.

My parents and brothers had arrived at the hotel room as I was showering. Mamá had brought my clothes in a bag. I was grateful she had thought to bring grandmother's hairbrush. I despaired for anything that would remind me of better days, of home and a family who truly loved me.

One of Rivas' goons, Matias, had stayed while I briefly reunited with my father and brothers. Papi looked handsome in his fine suit, as did my brothers. Papi and Mamá were so proud, and I lied when they asked me if I was happy.

"Yes, Mamá, Yes, Papi, I am happy. It's a good match and I will come to love Emmanuel as much as you both love each other." I knew it was a lie the minute the words left my lips. I gave my pleased father a kiss on the cheek, and hugged Mamá in my wedding gown.

"I have something for you, my Rosa." Mamá rustled in her purse and pulled out a small tissue-wrapped parcel. "You are almost perfect, little bride, but for one thing." Her frail, shaking fingers unwrapped the tissue, revealing a beautiful bright pink desert rose. She placed the little bloom in my hair, securing it with a pin.

"Perfect." Mam's eyes glistened with happy tears.

I felt my own tears break free, though they were far from joyful. I hugged her, trying not to ruin my makeup by weeping.

"Shh, pretty girl." Mamá dabbed at my mascara, cleaning up the dark smudges with the tissue her gift had been wrapped in.

Matias cleared his throat, tapping his watch. It was time to go to the courthouse where a judge would officiate at my wedding. The service was plain and simple, not how I would have wanted it had I been marrying my true love. Everything planned with Emmanuel's blessing, or not at all.

None of my friends were welcome at the small civil service. Heaven forbid, Eduardo might make an appearance. Rivas would make good on his promise. I had a feeling he was wondering how many more bullets my beloved might earn from the lies I told, or the truths I kept to myself.

My father stood with me as the Judge entered with Rivas, clapping a hand on the judge's shoulder and laughing. Rivas' eyes locked on mine, the possessive fire burned within the darkness and the corners of his lips quirked up in victory. The marriage was simply a formality; he had already taken me to his bed. Now he would possess me as his bride in the eyes of the law.

I glanced from my father to Mamá. She sat in a small chair, my brothers holding her hands. She was especially weak today. Something niggled in the back of my head

as I watched her. Her body shook with the effort it took to sit and pain was etched deeply into the lines and dark shadows haunting her eyes. My attention turned back to the judge who had begun. He didn't ask if I took this man to be my lawfully wedded husband. I was not asked to take any vows other than to honor, love and obey. I ducked my head in acknowledgment of the vows forced upon me by Rivas's iron grip tightening around my hands. I felt my knuckles shift painfully until I squeaked out an "I do." to each vow.

Rivas smiled, the light in his eyes dancing merrily. He finally possessed me. I wondered how long he had coveted me before he had made his move. His lips pressed against mine, his arms tightened around me, holding me tight against the hardness of his body. As much as I wanted to, I could not escape the vice-like grip of his arms as he held me, his wife.

The Devil had my hand in marriage,
but my punishment from God would be to
lose my mother, not three months later.

Chapter Six

I settled quietly into my new home. It had seven bedrooms, my own separate from Emmanuel's, for which I was grateful. There was an en suite bathroom through a door in my bedroom with a bathtub big enough for two people to enjoy. A modern kitchen occupied a large corner of the eastern side of the house. Tall windows framed the beautiful morning sunshine out over the far distant Sierras. The glistening reflection of a large kidney-shaped swimming pool danced over the walls of my room.

It was heaven in a gilded cage.

On our wedding night he barged into my room, again reeking of cheap perfume. He staggered to my bed, the stench of alcohol mingling with the heady scent of cheap floozy.

His hands pushed up the hem of my negligée, and pulled away the tiny scrap of lace which masqueraded as a pair of panties with a ridiculously expensive price tag. Lips, slippery with saliva, and breath reeking of cigars and alcohol slobbered over my skin. My flesh crawled as he leered over my body in the dim light. He moved his body over mine. His tongue felt slimy, licking in the dip at my throat before sliding over my collarbone and up my neck. Finally, over my jawline and onto my lips.

His hands clawed at my lace-covered breasts as he pressed his erection against me. I wriggled, a natural reaction to having such a foul creature pawing me. I was stopped by his hand tightening around my throat.

"Lay there, my beautiful wife…" he slurred. "Enjoy what I give you." He chuckled as he continued to kiss and lick at my face. His hand remained secure around

my throat, holding me in place, pinned like a
butterfly for display. His knees pushed
viciously at mine, spreading me for his
entrance. In his drunken state, he poked and
prodded my inner thighs, before grabbing
himself and pushing inside me. I sighed,
defeated, as my body accepted him. But
within my heart and soul, I would never
completely surrender.

I gasped at the intrusion, the invasion
of this man who was now my husband. He
thrust harder inside me, groaning in ecstasy.
I closed my eyes and allowed my thoughts
to drift to Eduardo.

My one and only bout of lovemaking
with Eduardo had been both pure and
beautiful. He had waited patiently to
penetrated me until I had turned eighteen.
He would never take my body like Rivas did
now. Heavy petting, kissing and soft
caresses of tongue to intimate places had

been heaven on earth. He would never and have been rough and manhandled me with such disrespect.

My breasts ached, and not with pleasure. Emmanuel thrust violently inside me, and I knew I would be battered and bruised tomorrow. I whimpered as the pain chased away my beautiful thoughts. This man was a monster of the purest and evillest kind. I had to find a way to escape.

***

Over the next few weeks, I was at the mercy of Emmanuel's lustful whims. Called into his office where the lingering smell of cheap perfume permeated everything around me. Some days it was a stale odour which lingered; other days more potent, as though his whore had been in the office just moments before I'd arrived. Sometimes, he forced me to wait while he finished a phone call. Sometimes, he would beckon me close while he talked and slip a hand under the skirts of my dress to slide his fingers through my folds. His touch elicited dual feelings of arousal and revulsion, the latter the stronger.

With each stroke of his finger inside my pussy, I plotted three things: my revenge, his death, and my escape. As soon as the first moan escaped my mouth and juice ran from me, he would finish his call and push me, stomach down, over his desk. My skirt was thrown over my ass and within seconds, his cock was freed and pushing inside me. I hated myself, so much more when I enjoyed the sexual stimulation.

It was a strange sensation, first a tingling then a rapture so great I couldn't stop the cry of pure bliss escaping my lips. His satisfied grunt as he climaxed, spilling his seed inside me, tore at my heart worse than when I had been told I was to marry him.

"I knew you would come around, Rosa. It was only a matter of time." He patted me on the head like I an obedient, well-trained bitch.

***

A week later, I was sitting at the breakfast bar in the kitchen when he appeared. His face somber when he joined me. I placed my coffee cup down, and cast my eyes over him.

For the past week, I had begged to see my family. When my beloved Mamá failed to contact me to inquire about my wedded, or not so wedded, bliss; I knew something was terribly wrong.

"So beautiful." He caressed my cheek. I lowered my head slightly, allowing his touch. It felt like a million slugs were attached to his fingers, causing my insides to curl with hatred. His hand slid from my cheek and I picked up the coffee cup again, bringing it to my lips.

"Your father called this morning. " He sucked in a deep breath. "Your mother has been taken to the hospital." I heard the words, knew their meaning, but my mind shut down when he explained my mother hadn't been responding at all to the treatment. Her body had begun to fail as cancer spread rapidly through her body. She had about a month left to live.

The cup slid from my hands, smashed against the marble countertop and the hot black contents spilled. I ignored the liquid as it dripped onto my white summer dress, some onto the clean white tiles beneath my seat. With my eyes glistening from unshed tears, I turned to the man who held the key to my cage.

"Emmanuel, please, I must go to her. I must be with her in her final month." The Devil's eyes had a strange cast to them. Empathy, sympathy, whatever it was I clutched at the humanity that surely lurked in the deep, darkness of his blackened soul.

"All right." He reached out and ran his fingertips along my knuckles. "You will have a bodyguard with you at all times." He raised my hand, his lips caressing my knuckles.

I nodded my agreement, grateful for the allowance.

The Devil did have some tiny sliver of heart.

Chapter Seven

I hate hospitals. A white, stark, sterile, soulless environment. The stench of bleach did its best to hide the aroma of illness, blood, urine and death. It failed miserably.

With a bunch of bright flowers clutched in my hand, I followed the corridor toward my mother's hospice care room. It would be here she would take her final breath, see the last rays of sunlight before God spirited her to his Kingdom to rest for eternity.

My two bodyguards stood outside the room as I busied myself beside Mamá's bed. I placed the flowers in a vase and helped her to sip at the juice box the nurse had left on her meal tray. This big city hospital was so much nicer, and more modern, than the simple clinic in our simple village.

Papi had returned to the village to work with Ricardo while Juan and I sat with Mamá. None of us wanted to be far from her. When my brother asked how my married life was, I smiled. Maurice and Manuel, my bodyguards, who were identical twins; would be listening at the half-open door and anything I said would be relayed back to my husband.

"Everything is wonderful. Emmanuel is amazing and so loving." I smiled, the lie fell easily from my lips. On hearing my lies, Mamá smiled. The light of joy in her eyes gave her hope that I was truly happy.

I returned home later that night to find a fourth bullet sitting on a silver tray with three others. My untrue words had indeed been relayed. He knew I was unhappy. I couldn't understand why he wanted me. Why keep an unhappy wife?

I was able to visit Mamá almost every day, returning each night to my bed. Sometimes, Emmanuel would claim me, the cheap perfume of his whore defiling my room before he defiled me.

I started to feel ill in the mornings before I left to go to Mamá's bedside. Panic gripped me. Emmanuel had said nothing about having children. How could I bear the Devil's child?

I visited the small drugstore by the hospital while my bodyguards waited. I used the guise of buying Mamá sweets, which I did. I also grabbed a pregnancy test, my heart sinking as the woman handed me the detailed receipt from the purchase.

While Mamá slept, I crept into the bathroom and took the test. Butterflies, more like wild horses stampeded in my stomach. My legs trembled and shook while I waited for the chemicals to work with my sample. The result would either doom me, or allow me to breathe normally again. I waited the minute and glanced at the stick. My heart stopped beating when I saw I was condemned.

I was carrying the Devil's baby.

***

Mamá's condition worsened day by day. I saw her watching me with a faint and knowing smile every time I had to excuse myself to the bathroom when morning sickness overwhelmed me. Emmanuel was far too busy conducting his business with the cartel to notice me, except at night when he fell upon me, using my body.

I felt no jealousy; how could I be jealous of a man I hated? I wished he would spend more time with his woman and leave me alone. My life would be so much happier without him. I could have been carrying my beloved Eduardo's baby. How I wished it was my beloved's child.

***

I awoke one night to hear the soft sobbing of a woman coming from down the hall. I rose and covered my body with a soft, silken robe. Barefoot, I padded softly down the hallway, following the sound which piqued my curiosity. Could this sobbing woman be the elusive whore my husband's body enjoyed before he came to my bed?

The light shone in his office, the door open. I hid from their sight.

"But Emmanuel, this baby, it is yours," the woman cried.

My breath hitched, did she know I was pregnant? Surely not. I didn't know who she was, had never seen her before in my life. I peeked through the door. Long dark curls bounced off her shoulders as she sobbed on her knees at my husband's feet. Her tanned skin appeared unblemished and perfect. Emmanuel glared down at her, seemingly bored with the drama playing out before him.

"You will get rid of it. I won't have a whore bearing a bastard of mine." He spoke cruelly.

Her sobbing hitched before her voice broke. "But you said you loved me, you would take care of me." Her head tilted as she looked up at him, her hands reaching for him, begging, pleading. "I can't get rid of the baby. I won't. He is our son. *Our son.*" She squealed as his hand gripped her hair, wrenching her head back.

"Now you listen to me, Melina." He lowered his head to her face, his lips an inch from hers "You have one chance at life, one only. My patience wears very thin. You will be rid of the bastard and then you will vanish. You will never approach me or any one of my men. From bodyguard, to drug runner, to dealer. Anyone in my Cartel so much as smells you, I will put a bullet between those fake breasts that you love me to suck and bite."

My eyes widened as he pulled out one of his gold-plated guns and ran the barrel down the terrified woman's cleavage.

"The boys here will take you to a clinic, and then you will get on a plane and go to America. What you do after that, I do not care." Emmanuel pushed her away roughly.

Melina sobbed, an emotional wreck on the floor. I started to pull away, unwilling to see her as she was hauled up by the twin guards. "No…" The soft word stopped me and I moved back. In some way, I was proud she had defied the Devil. But, I would learn later…….

You *never* cross the Devil.

The room became deathly quiet but for her sniffling.

"What did you say?" Emmanuel's voice dripped ice.

"I said, *no*." Melina tossed her hair away from her face with a flick of her head. "I will not kill our baby. I would rather die than kill an innocent child."

Emmanuel smirked. He stood from behind his desk and walked around to where the twins held Melina. "Then let me arrange it." Holding the gun, he walked back to the desk and opened a drawer. From within he pulled a cylinder, which he attached to the gun. A silencer.

"Adios, Melina. This is probably easier and cheaper than paying for your abortion." He lifted the gun and fired twice at her chest. Her body jerked with each shot before falling limp between the iron grip of the twins. Emmanuel smiled as he unscrewed the silencer and tucked his gun back in its holster. He crouched beside the corpse, caressed the curve of her breast and her face. Leaning forward, he kissed her one final time.

He casually pulled a cigar from his pocket, cut the end and lit it before turning to the twins. "Get rid of the bitch and make sure she's untraceable." He sat back and proceeded to enjoy the cigar.

I pulled away quickly. My heart hammered in my chest. I knew I had to escape. Somehow, I had to get away with my unborn baby and survive.

Chapter Eight

The last week of Mamá's life flew by in a blur of doctors and nurse visits. Emmanuel visited me nightly, but no longer did he stink of cheap perfume. Now he had the rich smell of cigars; no less sickening to my sensitive stomach. The memory of what he had done to his mistress, and how callous he had been, was forever burned into my memory.

I had sent my beloved a note via my youngest brother, Juan, who was still attending school in the village. In the note, I explained my fears and my condition. He was the only person privy to my pregnancy though I knew Mamá suspected. The next morning Juan handed me a small slip of paper when he came in to visit with Mamá.

"My beloved,

We must run away, as soon as it is possible. You must get away from him, he is a very dangerous man. I have friends in America, where I went to college. They will hide us until we can make a place for ourselves, free and safe from him. When the time is right, I will come for you. I love you, no matter the child you carry is not mine. I will love this child as if it were my own and be a father he, or she, can be proud of.

-Eduardo.''

I held the note to my chest, hot tears of joy and hope trickled down my face. We would make it, we *had* to.

I returned home to find a party in full swing. Loud Latin music pumped from the expensive stereo. Its beat pounding through every cell in my body in an irritating way. Women with their breasts exposed danced for the men, some even writhed naked on the laps of Emmanuel's men as the music pulsed. Fine lines of white powder lay on small square mirrors with razors and rolled up notes and straws beside them.

I watched as one woman rolled up an American banknote and held it to her nose, inhaling a line of pure white before she tipped her head back and sighed with bliss. She was grabbed roughly by one of the men and hauled up to dance. The term dancing, I use very loosely, for as I passed the living room, he pushed her skirt up, revealing she wore no panties. He fumbled with his pants, she moaned loud enough for all to hear as he pushed himself inside her.

I turned away from the scene of debauchery and excess to make my way to my room, my sanctuary. I was desperate for a hot shower and peace to plan my escape. Peace I most likely would not get this night. "Rosa!" A familiar voice called to me. I stopped in my tracks, my heart pounding in fear. I turned, seeing my best friend, Emilia staggering toward me. Her eyes were too bright and her breath reeked of alcohol.

"Isn't this great?" Her words slurred as she spoke. I placed my arms around her unsteady form in an attempt to stabilize her, a difficult task considering the high stilettoes she wore. She was six months younger than me and should not have been drinking. She shouldn't have been at this party, or near these people.

"Emi, what are you doing here?" I asked as she stumbled into me. I gripped her shoulders, steadying her.

"Partying, Rosa. I got invited by one of the hunks over there." She giggled and pointed her drink-holding hand to the small bar where Dante was pouring more liquor into glasses.

"Emi, you need to listen to me right now. This is not a good place for you to be, these are bad men here." I pleaded with her, trying to break through the teenage rebel I held in my arms.

"Why? I was invited. If you don't like them, go home." She giggled and stumbled. "Oh wait, you are home.! I didn't even get to be your maid of honor, what kind of best friend are you, huh?" She pushed me away and slurped her drink as she staggered backward. "I'm going to go find new friends."

"Emi, wait…" I tried to grab her, but she pushed me away, staggering into the welcoming arms of one of Emmanuel's men. It was no use; my best friend had been seduced by the Devil's men. Was there no part of my life he did not touch and destroy? I turned sadly and trudged up the stairs to my room.

I stripped my clothes and showered. My mind sorted through plans of escape before scrapping them because I knew they wouldn't work. If anything, we needed to escape over the border. *El Grito de Independencia* was coming in a few months, it would provide a distraction. Perhaps, during the festival of Mexico's independence, I could find my own with my beloved Eduardo.

I rinsed my hair before massaging a conditioner through it. Steam swirled around my body as I toweled myself dry. I looked at myself in the mirror. My eyes appeared haunted with sorrow. Misery, my companion where love should have held sway. Beyond that, there lay hope. A tiny spark which I hoped very soon would blossom into a full shine. My hands drifted to the tiny life within my belly. I wanted nothing but the best for this child, and that included a life away from the Devil, even if he was this babe's father.

What he had done to his mistress had proven, he was not fit to be a father, let alone breathe the same air this child would one day breathe. I slipped a nightgown over my body and left the bathroom. Manuel stood by the entry to my room.

"What do you want?" My surprise was evident in the rudeness in which I spoke.

"The Boss would like to see you in his office, Rosa." He smirked as his eyes perused my body.

I sighed and slipped a silk bathrobe around my body. Manuel escorted me to my husband's office where I heard the soft gasps and moans of a woman. I stopped and glanced at Manuel who winked knowingly.

He knocked on the door and Emmanuel's voice called for us to enter, the gasps and impassioned moans never halting for a moment. Manuel pushed open the door.

The air rushed from my lungs as I witnessed the scene before me. Emilia was bent over the desk, naked. Her breasts pooled on the mahogany desktop, her mouth open in a perfect circle of ecstasy. Her beautiful eyes closed as my husband thrust inside her. He slowed, putting his hand on her back, holding Emi in place.

"Ah, Rosa, Manuel here tells me that you didn't want to join the party downstairs?" He ceased thrusting to pick up a glass of liquor. He shifted his hips, making Emi moan underneath him while he sipped his drink. "So, I thought we could have our own, *private* party." He grinned, licking the liquor from his lips before he set the glass down again. I lowered my eyes to the carpet, Manuel backed away and closed the door.

"Come here," my husband commanded.

I folded my arms across my chest and shook my head.

"Come, sweet one, come play." His voice took on a harder, demanding edge.

I looked up at him. His eyes were hard, dark with lust and desire.

To my horror, Emi gazed at me from her position on the desk. "Come on, Rosa. Come and play with us." She smiled.

I noticed the crust of white under her nostril. Her eyes were glazed and she was pale. "What have you given her?"

"Something to help her enjoy the party." Emmanuel rolled his hips, his cock deep inside my best friend. "Get up on the desk. I won't ask you again, *wife*." He gripped Emi's hips and dragged her from the desk, holding her upright while I moved between them and the desk.

"Take off your clothes." Emmanuel sat in his chair, Emi still impaled on his cock. She wriggled in his lap, giggling. I heard the sharp crack as his hand met with her ass. Emi gave a short yelp then moaned as Emmanuel thrust deeper inside her.

Emi giggled when Emmanuel ran a hand over her pert breasts, his eyes watching me darkly as I slowly tugged the silken tie from my robe. He slowly shifted his hips, thrusting inside my best friend as I let the robe slip from my shoulders to pool at my feet. I slid the shoulder straps off my body, letting my negligee float to the floor.

"On the desk, Rosa." I slowly slid my bottom over the desk, ignoring the little mirror with the lines of Cocaine cut neatly like bars of a prison. "Spread your legs, and lean back on your hands." He ordered. I slowly moved into position, resting my upper body weight on the desktop.

"Good girl," Emmanuel purred. Now, little girl, taste my wife." He gripped Emi's hair and pushed her face to the place between my legs.

I whimpered with revulsion when Emi's mouth made contact with my pussy. Her tongue slid between the lips of my folds, and I jumped in fright at the contact of another woman's mouth against my intimate place. Emmanuel continued to thrust slowly, pushing Emi's mouth harder against my pussy.

I squealed when I felt the sharpness of her teeth slice against my clit. White flashes of pain strobed behind my tightly shut eyelids as I placed my hand between her mouth and my injured womanhood. The pain so great, I curled into a ball and slid from the desk. I barely registered Emmanuel's cruel laughter which was cut short by Emi's pain-filled shriek and the hard crack of a hand striking flesh.

I panted in pain as my body throbbed. Emi whimpered and fell in a heap beside me.

"Stupid bitch, can't even lick a cunt properly."

I was dragged to my feet by Emmanuel, his cock brushing against my stomach, leaving a smear of Emi's juices on my skin.

"Did she hurt you?" He ran his fingers from my cheek, over my breasts and stomach, to my stinging clit, I bit back a whimper of pain and nodded, knowing the tone of his voice demanded an answer. A truthful one.

"Fucking whore." He spat and held me against his side as he stepped closer to Emi's cowering form. He pulled a leg back and kicked her, his body jolting mine with the impact. Emi screamed, and continued to scream as he booted her, ignoring my pleas for him to stop his assault on her.

His breathing was hard and heavy by the time Emi's cries turned to quiet whimpers. "Put your clothes back on and go to bed." He voice was soft and deadly as sin. I nodded, my eyes stinging from the tears and my throat strained from my cries for mercy on Emi's behalf. Emmanuel watched as I gingerly moved, each step sending pain shooting to the injured bundle of nerves. I pulled the robe on, grabbed the discarded negligee and left my husband as he leaned back in his chair and lit a cigar.

One of his men entered as I reached the door. I closed it softly, to the chilling orders from my husband. "Get rid of this whore, but have some fun with her first." The Devil had stolen my best friend.

Chapter Nine.

I sat in the small hospice room where my mother lay in the last stage of cancer. She had slipped into a coma earlier.

The night of Mexico's Independence Day was only hours away. My little brother had handed me the final note in my exchanges with Eduardo. Tonight, was to be our escape. Tonight, we would be free.

I placed a hand over my stomach, my little one was growing and soon the bump would be noticeable. I was two days from the end of the first trimester, and I had managed to hide my condition. When I was free, I would visit a doctor and have regular check-ups to ensure my baby was healthy and happy.

As the darkness grew, Mamá's breaths became shallower. Her body began shutting down and the doctors said she would only have a few days at best to live. I sat by her bedside and whispered to her about the escape plan, how unhappy I was in my marriage and how cruel my husband

was. I explained much I loved Eduardo, and how, if the baby was a girl, we would name the child after her. I was certain I felt her squeeze my hand gently at that news.

The sound of celebrations outside the hospital grew louder. I knew the time was coming. Emmanuel wanted me back at the house for a party. I was hoping, by the time they discovered I was gone, he would be too drunk, high or cock deep in the next whore to care until he sobered up.

There was a soft knock at the door, Juan entered and nodded. The plan was in motion. One of the nurses had lured my bodyguard away, and was currently entertaining him in one of the supply closets. I stood, kissed my Mamá goodbye for the last time and followed my brother out of her room. I could not look back, for to do so, would make me stay until she took her last breath, and I could not do that and have my chance at freedom.

Juan guided me past the closet where the soft moans of the nurse could be heard as she gave herself to Dante. My brother led me to a service entry, where Eduardo was waiting with a friend of his in an old pickup. He pulled me into a tight and loving embrace, his lips taking mine with passion, desire, and deep love never shown in my marriage.

"Quickly, Rosa, into the back." Eduardo helped me into the bed of the truck. He climbed in after me and covered us both with an old oiled tarp. I held his hand as the pickup started up, the old engine rumbling loudly as my heartbeat pounded in my chest in fear. The old vehicle rumbled out of the hospital grounds, down the road and out of town. I jumped when I heard the first gunshots.

"Shh, my love, it is only the fireworks." Eduardo lifted a corner of the tarp so we could see the beautiful colors exploding and lighting up the night sky.

I smiled, and snuggled against him, celebrating the first leg of our journey to freedom.

He held me close through the night as we lay safely tucked away in the pickup truck. We traveled for hours until we reached a place where the patrols along the Mexico/US border were paid well to look the other way.

"Hey, time to go lovebirds." The driver tapped the side of the pickup.

Eduardo pulled the tarp from our bodies. It was near dawn with a faint line of red glowing in the east. We didn't have much time.

Eduardo's friend handed him a bag. "Passports, identifications, social security numbers, all should pass inspection. There's even a marriage certificate. So, congratulations Mr. and Mrs Corso." He chuckled.

"Thank you, my friend." Eduardo smiled and clasped the man's hand in a handshake.

"Just be safe, and make sure you have a room for me when I come visit."

"We will." Eduardo took the bag. "Come, my love, we have to go before the patrols come through." He led the way toward a section of the fence. He gripped the fence and pulled it back, revealing a large hole. "Go, Rosa, run to the bushes and I'll be with you in a moment."

My heart pounded with excitement and terror. I slipped through the fence. My feet felt like they barely touched the ground as I raced across the earth. The bushes scratched and tore at my skin as I passed. I skidded to a stop in the safety of their branches, out of breath and panting. I waited for Eduardo, almost shrieking with fright when he slid up behind me.

"Are you ready to start a new life, my love?" He gathered me in his arms.

"Yes, yes my love." I cried softly, feeling safe and secure in his arms. Our future looked so very bright

I had escaped the Devil

I moved quickly to fill the orders in the small diner which was surrounded by large, ugly skyscrapers. It was cozy and proudly shouted 'Small Town USA' which busy people in suits seemed to love. I moved quickly to clear the tables that were vacated so more customers could flood in. A Latino man sat down and looked over the menu. There was something about him which caused my skin to tingle, I wanted to get home to see my baby.

It had been a year since Eduardo and I had escaped. We lived in a small onebedroom apartment in a very poor area. He worked at a local high school as a janitor during the day and cleaned offices at night. With my waitressing job, we scraped by.

Our daughter, Isabella, named after my mother, was six months old and growing like a beautiful flower. A girl who lived in our building took care of her when I was at work. It had taken me a long time to take a chance and seek work, and it was so hard to be away from my baby.

I looked to the man at my table, "What can I get you, sir?" I said in my accented English.

"Coffee, black, no sugar, Rosie." He said. I startled, wondering how he knew my name, but then I recalled, I had a name badge on my uniform.

"Coming right up, sir," I said with a smile I didn't feel. I left to get the man's order, and on the way back, a customer bumped into me, causing me to spill the coffee over my uniform. "Oh, I'm so sorry sir, please let me clean that up," I said as I grabbed a clean cloth from behind the counter and attempted to mop up the coffee I'd spilled over him.

"It's all right, it was my fault, I'm sorry, I should have been watching what I was doing."

I quickly grabbed another coffee for the customer whose coffee I had spilled, only to find him gone. I glanced around the small diner but couldn't sight him at all. I shook my head and placed the coffee on the table. A tiny pink flower lay upon a neatly folded napkin. *A Desert Rose*.

Coffee dampened my pastel pink diner uniform, so I left to clean up. In the employee bathroom, I patted myself dry with paper towels and noticed, my name badge was missing.

I was on edge for the rest of my shift; something wasn't right. My knees jittered as

I sat on the subway, feet hurting from being on them all day, my uniform a mess from the spilled coffee and some sixth sense nagging at me to get home, quickly.

I left the subway station and hurried through the streets, heading to the apartment complex which housed our building. Our little home.

We'd had nothing but the clothes on our backs and a thousand American dollars to our name, but it was enough to pay two months' rent and get the utilities connected. Soon a mattress and then a bed frame were added to our bedroom. A worn couch and a rickety kitchen table followed. At Goodwill, we managed to get clothes and linens for our home, and a neighbor had kindly given us an old crib that they would never need again.

Our little home was not luxurious, but it was more home to me than a seven-bedroom mansion with a modern kitchen and a kidney shaped pool.

I raced up the five flights of stairs as the elevator was broken. The building manager never seemed to care to fix it. I pulled keys from my bag as I walked along the worn and stained carpet, ignoring the graffiti-lined walls and the stench of marijuana and urine as I reached apartment 5D, home.

I slid the key into the lock and opened the door. The apartment was dark, quiet.

"Yolanda?" I called out, wondering where the babysitter was. "Yolanda, I'm home." I stepped into my apartment, letting the door close behind me. I rushed through the short hall and turned into the kitchen. It was dark, the blinds drawn. Frantically, I checked through the apartment. I found the blinds drawn in the living room and our bedroom door was closed. I was certain I'd left it open when I'd left Yolanda to care for Isabella. I heard something moving in the kitchen; my heart rate spiked as I turned back to the kitchen doorway.

"Hello?" I squinted into the darkness. My hand reached around to the light switch. I flicked it on, and the air left my lungs. My heart thundered in my chest; I shook uncontrollably as absolute terror flowed through my body.

"Hello, darling." Emmanuel held my daughter in his arms as he sat at the old kitchen table. "Been playing happy families without me, have you?"

My hand flew to my mouth as I watched him stand with my child in his arms, my eyes never leaving the sweet sleeping face of my little angel.

I stepped backward as he approached me. My back slammed against a wall of muscle, and strong hands gripped my shoulders, preventing further retreat.

"Please, please don't hurt her, Emmanuel. She is our daughter."

He smirked, and peered down at the little girl in his arms.

"Yes, I know." He looked back at me, a dark smile on his face.

The Devil had my daughter.

Chapter Eleven.

Isabella shifted and whimpered in Emmanuel's arms. "Shh, hush little one." He crooned. "Mamá and Papi are just going to have a chat."

I was pushed forward. Emmanuel shifted Isabella into the crook of one arm and guided me to sit down, his hand in the small of my back as tears broke free. I tried to be brave, but I knew we were in serious trouble, now Emmanuel had found us. I knew he was never going to let me, or our baby, go.

"Where's the babysitter?" I asked after I managed to get my sobs under control.

"She's entertaining the twins, in your room." Emmanuel glanced at me briefly before returning his attention to the baby he rocked gently in his arms. I swallowed, knowing Yolanda would be barely recognizable if she survived the twin's attentions.

"Ahh, my beautiful wife, for a year I have been searching for you." He reached out to caress my face. I flinched and tried to pull away, only to have him grip my chin, digging his fingernails into my skin. "And where do I find you? In a shit hole of an apartment, surrounded by filth and whores?" His voice was angry, and if it were possible, I was certain steam would be shooting out of his ears.

"Where is the fucker who took you from me?" He stood quickly, jostling Isabella who whimpered and began to cry. Emmanuel soothed her, putting her up on his shoulder as if he had been with her throughout the first six months of her life. He patted her little back, soothing her. She continued to cry before her little voice hiccupped and she calmed.

"Eduardo is at work." I peered down at my hands before looking up at my baby in the hands of her sadistic father. I feared for my baby, my lover, my own life. I would give Emmanuel my miserable life if it meant the two most important, and beloved people in my life were spared the Devil's wrath. "Please, Emmanuel, don't hurt him, or Isabella." I pleaded and dropped to my knees. My hands clasped together, and I begged as I lowered my head in supplication. My heart broke as I watched his face twist into an evil smile. This man had no sense of mercy.

"My darling wife, why should I spare that bastards life? He stole you and our baby away from me. You do recall the promise I made the day before our wedding?" He crouched down to lift my chin so I could look at him. I tried hard to avoid his evil gaze, but he forced me to look at him.

"Y-yes." Hot tears of misery flowed over my face and his fingers as he held me.

"Good." He smiled before he leaned in and kissed me. I recoiled, but his hand moved to the back of my head and forced me into the kiss, my teeth clashed against his and his slimy tongue pushed past my lips seeking entry past the barrier of my teeth. I refused to open my mouth to let him in. He sucked my bottom lip between his teeth and bit down hard, drawing blood and tearing the delicate soft flesh inside my lip. I cried out with the pain, he took advantage, kissing me with savage possession. He pushed me away, I fell backward and collapsed onto the floor. He grabbed the telephone off the kitchen table and dropped it on the floor beside me.

"Call his work, tell them he needs to come home immediately, there's something wrong with the baby."

I held a hand to my mouth, tasting blood. It dripped down my chin to splatter the floor in little droplets mixed with my saliva. I shook my head. "I-I-I can't." I sobbed.

Emmanuel smiled, before he pulled one of his gold-plated pistols from its holster, cocked it and pointed it at Isabella's head.

"Do it, or there *will* be something wrong with the child." His voice was cold, emotionless and his eyes bore a darkness even I never knew he possessed. I was shocked he would draw a gun on his own innocent child.

"Please, don't do this," I whispered.

"I haven't done this, Rosa. This is all *your* doing. Every part has been played by your hand. Now call him." He cocked the gun, pressing it against my baby's forehead.

My eyes red raw and still weeping, I picked up the phone and called the office building where Eduardo worked.

"Simmons and Simmons and Associates, Security desk, Clive speaking." The voice of the friendly, elderly security officer, who had come to our poor apartment for dinner a few times, greeted me. I could hear the humming of the vacuum cleaner in the background.

"Hello, Clive, this is Rosie Corso. Can you please tell Eduardo to come home, right away? Our baby is sick, and I need to get her to a hospital."

"He's right here, Rosie, just a sec." I heard the vacuum cleaner being shut off in the background.

"Rosie, what's wrong baby? Is Isabella okay?" Eduardo sounded concerned.

"No." I sobbed, my heart heavy with guilt. "I don't know what's wrong with her. She has a high fever, and I don't know what to do. Please, I need you to come home, I have to get her to a hospital."

"Ok my love, I will be there soon, just hold tight. I love you."

"I love you too," I whispered before hanging up the phone.

"Good girl." Emmanuel smiled, patting my head.

"Now, we wait." The door to my bedroom clicked open, and the twins came out, looking mighty pleased with themselves. One of them tossed a used needle back into the bedroom.

"How was she?" Emmanuel asked, ignoring me as I wept silently on the floor.

"Virginal and perfect. She's sleeping. The heroin will work its magic and she won't wake up." Maurice grinned, as he fiddled with the cuffs on his shirt.

Manuel grinned and finished buckling his belt. I felt sick to my stomach at the thought of what they had done to the poor girl. She didn't deserve this, to be abused and murdered. Emmanuel was right, I had brought this all on myself, my family and my friends.

"I'm glad you had fun," Emmanuel smirked.

It was twenty minutes before
Eduardo burst through the front door to our
apartment.

Emmanuel greeted his breathless face
with a loaded pistol. "Ah, the happy family
is complete." He grinned maliciously as he
held me in one arm, and cuddled our baby
tight to his chest. "You have taken the two
most precious things of mine. My wife." He
turned his head and kissed me. "And my
daughter." He leaned down, at the same time
raising up Isabella to place a soft kiss to her
forehead. She gurgled in his arms. "That's
right, little Bella, Papi's got you now, and

he will never let you go." He turned his
attention back to Eduardo, who was now
being held tightly by the twins.

"Let's go." He pulled me forward
after he holstered his gun.

My footsteps were heavy. Eduardo's eyes caught mine, his eyes were full of sorrow, and one thing I did not expect, forgiveness. "Torch this shithole," Emmanuel said as we walked out the front door. I could smell the gasoline before we got to the end of the hallway.

He loaded me into his limousine, while Eduardo was hauled into the back of a black van. Emmanuel held me tight against him as we drove out of the city. Our precious little girl slept in his other arm. Dante sat opposite us, his hand never straying far from his holstered gun.

"At ease, Dante," he chuckled. "I do not think that Rosa will be so foolish as to risk Isabella's life. Would you, my little desert rose?"

I shook my head in misery. "No."

"Good girl." He tucked me tighter against him, kissing my forehead. I felt as though I was being crushed, certain I could feel my ribs shifting.

"We have one more stop before we head home, my love." We drove out of the city, traveling for hours until we turned off the highway onto a small country road which led to a National Forest.

My heart pounded harder as I watched the van pull up in front of us and the twins drag a beaten and bloodied Eduardo out.

The Devil had plans for us.

Chapter Twelve

Dante helped me from the car. Emmanuel handed Isabella to him and grabbed me by the arm. Eduardo was bound hand and foot. The twins dragged him to a patch of dirt and tossed his beaten form to the ground.

"Stand him up," Emmanuel ordered the twins.

Eduardo cried out as they grabbed him roughly and forced him to stand. His left shoulder sagged from dislocation, his nose had been broken, blood streamed over his beautiful lips and stained his janitor's uniform. One eye was already swollen shut, and the other was not far from joining it. It almost destroyed me, seeing him this brutalized. I turned to my husband.

"Please, Emmanuel. Please let him go. Isabella and I will go with you willingly. I beg you, don't kill him."

He turned to me, his face a mask of emotionlessness. "My beloved Rosa, don't worry, I won't kill him."

I sighed softly, the relief coursing through me. He gathered both my hands in his, bringing them to his soft lips and kissing them before the words that would crush me were spoken. "You will."

"No… please no." I screamed in anguish.

"Oh yes, my darling. And you *will* use every bullet you earned."

He held up one hand and with the other marked off his fingers:

"One for telling me there were no other lovers in your life. Two for telling me your lover was just a friend. Three for giving him your virginity when it belonged to me. Four for telling your dying whore of a mother you were happy and five for not telling me you were pregnant."

He changed hands and counted off the other fingers. "Six for leaving me. Seven for hiding. Eight for not returning to me where you belong and two more because I feel like it." He dragged me forward to face Eduardo's unsteady form.

"Please, Emmanuel, don't make me do this. I can't, I won't. I'd rather die." He stood me before my lover, his hand taking mine and carefully wrapping my fingers around the handle of one of his gold-plated pistols. I felt his warm chest pressing against my back, his hand raising mine, controlling me like a puppet on a deadly string.

"Put your finger on the trigger, my love." His voice was cold, hard in my ear, a contrast to the warm breath.

"*No!*" I shook my head and fought against my husband. Emmanuel brought his other hand up, caging me in his arms, he coaxed my unwilling fingers into a position, index on the trigger, while the other supported the instrument of death.

"Now, my darling, we are going to put the first bullet in his left shoulder, the second in his right. Third and fourth in his kneecaps, fifth into his cock, sixth into his gut, seventh into his heart, eighth into his head and…" He paused. "Two more in his cock for putting it where it didn't belong." He murmured instructions into my ear.

My body shook with abject fear. "I won't do this," I lowered my head and attempted to lower the gun, but Emmanuel's arms were stronger than mine. I couldn't force myself away from him.

"Shh, sweet one. If he doesn't take the bullets at your hand, your family will by mine. And, what of Isabella? Does she not deserve to live?"

I sobbed, knowing he would make good on his promise to kill the last members of my family.

"Rosa, do it. It's all right, I love you. I forgive you. We will meet again, I promise." Eduardo's broken voice carried to my ears like an angel.

"No, I can't."

"Yes, you can. It's alright. I'm ready. I am so grateful I had you for….." the words died on his lips as the first gunshot rang out.

I hadn't even realized that Emmanuel had pushed gently on my finger, squeezing the trigger and condemning me to kill the one I love. My entire body jerked backward into Emmanuel with the kick of the pistol.

"That's one." He whispered.

I could barely hear him over Eduardo's screams, as he writhed on the ground. Isabella's cries at being woken up by the loud noise of the gun firing tore through my near shattered defenses.

"Put my daughter in the car," Emmanuel instructed Dante.

Isabella's cries muffled when the door to the limo was closed. I breathed a tiny sigh of relief.

"Next one, darling." He moved me closer to Eduardo's body as he lay in pain.

Blood seeped from the bullet wound in his shoulder. We stood over him, my husband, the Devil behind me. His hands steadied my shaking hands as he pressed my finger again, forcing me to curl it against the trigger. Together we squeezed the next rounds from the gun, eliciting another cry from Eduardo.

Emmanuel forced me to look upon my lover's body as he exchanged the empty gun for another. Two more shots pierced his already shattered cock, he didn't scream, he was almost at Heaven's door. He was barely breathing, but his eyes flickered open and locked with mine. Love and forgiveness shone through the agony.

"I love you." He whispered before Emmanuel lifted the gun fired into Eduardo's skull. His body jerked, he was dead. Released from the pain I have brought down on him.

I was frozen to the spot, shaking but numb. Emmanuel kissed my neck, his hands running over my body and a sickening erection pressed against my ass. He led me back to the limo, left our daughter in the care of Dante and ordered him to take her to the van which had delivered Eduardo.

I didn't care when I was pushed into the limo. I felt the slice of the knife against my skin as my panties were cut free and my husband slammed his cock deep inside me. The limo rocked as I was taken.

***

We had been travelling for hours before I could look up at my murderous husband and asked the one burning question I should have asked from the beginning.

"Why did you marry me?" I asked, facing him from the opposite seat in the limousine

He looked at me, his eyes hard, deadly as he gently rocked our sleeping daughter in his arms.

"A few years ago, your grandfather backed out of a very lucrative deal that could have kept your family fed and living well. But he decided to cross me, and the Cartel. I made a decision as to his fate, and the fate of your family for his foolish choice." Isabella woke and burbled a little in his arms, he gently rocked her and hushed the previous babe. "I wanted to take from him something that was indeed precious. His family." He looked at me again.

"You are a possession for me to keep, your mother knew you were unhappy before she died, you family are in debit to me, you father borrowed money off me to keep his house, but I now own it, and he and your brothers work for me." He cooed at his daughter as her hands reached up and tried to grab his nose. His lips pressed softly at one chubby fist. "I never had love for your, Rosa, or your family. I think you know this."

It was the first time I ever saw the man show any affection towards anything.

"And Isabella? Are you going to allow her life to be as miserable as mine and my family's?" I asked him.

"No, she is the exception, she is mine." He smiled down at her. "She will be happy, she will be loyal, and loved, unlike her mother." Emmanuel glared at me.

"From now on, my darling wife, you will not take a shit without my knowledge. Dante will be your shadow. I will provide you with whatever you require in life, but you will never, ever leave me again. If you do, I will wipe out your entire family before I finally find you and make our daughter do to you what you have done to your lover."

He leaned forward, Isabella reaching up to grab at the collar of his shirt where there was a tiny splatter of Eduardo's blood marring the pristine white linen.

"Do you understand me, Rosa?"

"Yes, Emmanuel." I whispered, my voice tight my body numb with the terrorising thought of my baby holding a gun to my head at the urging of her father.

"Good." He looked back down to Isabella, who had become fussy.

I slowly reached inside the baby bag which held her bottle of formula and a pack of diapers. "Would you like to feed her?" I asked, taking out the bottle. It had stayed warm in the limo, perfect for Isabella. I handed it to him, and watched as he seemed to struggle slightly with feeding her before I moved over to sit beside him, my hand guiding his with the bottle to our daughter's mouth, as he had guided mine with his pistol to take my lover's life.

In his touch, I knew the truth.

I was the Devil's Possession

Epilogue.

The beautiful sun shone over the gardens as I poured myself yet another glass of liquor. Much of my days were spent in a drunken stupor, trying to destroy the memories of the past, of Eduardo.

My four-year-old daughter, Isabella, chased a butterfly, while the nanny, whom I knew my husband was fucking every chance he got, watched over her.

As promised, Dante was my constant shadow. I lifted the glass to my lips, wincing slightly as the stitches in my wrists pulled with the movements. The stark white bandages were a reminder of my failure to leave this world, this life under the Devil.

"Bella!" the familiar and hated voice called out over the garden.

"Papi!" my baby cried joyfully as Emmanuel walked on to the neatly trimmed grass. He scooped Isabella into his arms and spun her around. She giggled.

She was beautiful. She was my baby.

In the arms of the Devil.